Emma Comes to Maine

By Julie Patten

Illustrated by Elsie Drummond

Published by Piscataqua Press
an imprint of RiverRun Bookstore

ISBN: 978-1-950381-59-3

To all those who provide
loving homes for animals
who need rescuing.

Who I Am

I'm a beagle. And that should tell you just about everything there is to know about me. I'm always happy, I love people, and I follow my nose. No matter what kind of pens or cages people shut me up in, I always manage to escape. For the first five years of my life, that's exactly what I did.

Escaping isn't all fun and games,

though. I got to run free, but I had to

forage for food and never had a place

to call home. I didn't have a bed to

sleep in or a warm cozy person to

snuggle up with.

As I got older, I grew tired of this

routine. I would be picked up by a stranger, taken to a new place and then locked up. I was always alone. I hated my small pens and had to work very hard to break out of them. Things were always changing, and I could never really settle down. I didn't have anyone to call my friend.

The last time I got captured was different, though. A big guy in a uniform with a badge picked me up. He took me in his car, which had a light on top, to a cement building with people working at desks and

chairs. He was very nice to me and petted me a lot instead of sticking me in a pen outside and ignoring me like everyone else in my life had done. He gave me lots of treats and led me to a big puffy bed by his desk so I could lie down. He took me out for short walks on a leash to do my business. There was no chance this time for me to dig out and run loose.

Only a few days passed before a van with a lot of other dogs came to pick me up. The driver was very nice. He put me in my own separate cage, just

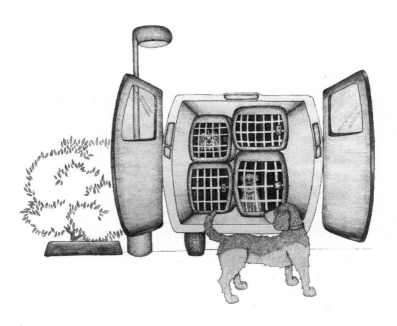

like all the other dogs. I had no idea what the plan was, but, then again, I didn't have much choice. I went from leash to cage and then sat for a pretty long drive — really long, it seemed. I was tired and hot and bored. Finally, when we stopped, there were many different people there waiting for us with cars and leashes and bowls of water and treats! It was unlike anything I had seen before.

A man and woman came up to me right away and hugged me and fussed over me. It felt different but good.

They kept petting me and holding me and petting me more. It almost seemed as if they couldn't get enough of me. The driver gave them some paperwork and chatted a bit and sent the three of us off. The man and woman put a bright red collar around my neck and attached a pretty, new red leash to it and led me to their car. First, they offered me some water and gave me some treats. Then they helped me into the back of their car. It had a lot of space.

We drove for a while, but it didn't seem too long because I was very tired, and I guess I slept. I woke suddenly, though, when the woman sitting in the front seat yelled, "Look at the sign, Emma. It says, 'Welcome to Maine'!" She went on. "You're in your new home. Things will be very different for you from now on." I didn't quite follow what she was saying, but she sure was excited.

It wasn't long before we pulled into the driveway of a big yellow house. My new people let me out of the car, never letting go of my new leash, and

brought me inside. There was plenty of room for me to sniff around and lots of new stuff I wasn't used to. A big fluffy cushion was on the floor with lots of toys nearby. When I went over to the cushion, they said, "Good girl." They spoke in such a nice tone of voice and I really liked that. I wasn't especially used to it either. In the past, I was either ignored or scolded.

Next thing I knew, they kept saying, "Emma." Every time they looked at me or seemed to be talking about me, they said, "Emma." I heard it so much that I was becoming used to it. I kind of liked it. They said it so gently and they especially said it when they were petting me.

My new people didn't take me outside and push me into a pen or cage only to shut the door and leave me there. Instead, they led me outside with them into their big backyard. They unhooked my leash from my new collar. *Ooooh, this looks like fun,* I thought. I was free to roam! I darted away from them, but immediately came to a fence. I ran along the edge

of the fence, hoping to escape, but

the fence kept going and going. It was

like a big circle attached to the house

at either end. It was a high fence, but

you could see through it and I thought

it wouldn't be hard to dig under, so

I tried. It didn't work, though. They

had rocks buried under the fence so there really wasn't any way for me to dig out. This was all new to me. I had always managed to escape.

The other thing that was different was they hung out with me. They ran with me and called me and clapped their hands and when I came to them, they gave me treats. They let me in their house all the time, and I could sleep practically wherever I wanted. They gave me a bed in the same room where they slept with my own blanket and stuffed toy. They talked to me.

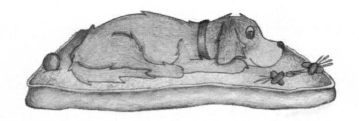

They hugged me. They petted me.

They fed me twice a day in a dish they had in a special place. There was a bowl always full of water for me,too. I wasn't used to getting meals on a regular basis,and it took some getting used to, but it didn't take long for me to know what time I'd be getting a yummy meal. I always ate it all and licked the bowl until it was totally clean. Then they praised me and even gave me a treat afterwards they called "dessert." More fun was coming my way all the time!

The weather was getting warmer, and we spent more and more time outside together. They took me for walks in the woods behind their house on my brand-new red leash. My man person — who I was beginning to know as "Dad" — would walk me in

the morning and my woman person — who I was beginning to know as "Mom" — would walk me every afternoon. It was fun. I saw turkeys and deer and all sorts of other animals. I wanted to chase them, but my mom or dad held tight to that leash, so I couldn't take off like I used to do. At first it was frustrating, but the more I got used to it, the more I kind of liked being attached to the same people and routine. I was beginning to feel secure in my new life in Maine and didn't even want to try to run away anymore.

Doggy Day Scare

One day, Mom put on my leash and said, "Come on, Emma, let's get in the car." For a second, I got a little scared. Being in a car brought back memories of long trips to unknown places. She kept talking to me in a calm voice saying, "It's okay, Emma. We're going to a place where you can play with other dogs for the day. It'll be fun!"

I didn't know what she was saying, but after a short drive, she led me into a building where there were lots of barking dogs. There were big dogs and little dogs and people playing with them. There was a big inside room and a big fenced-in yard. She talked with a girl and then petted me on my head and said goodbye to me. I was sad. I didn't understand at all. Was she taking me away from my new life in the big yellow house? What about my man person who walked me in the mornings? I didn't like this. The girl took me by my leash and led me into a big room with other dogs who were running around playing.

There were a few big cushions scattered around on the floor and I headed for one of those to sit and watch. A middle-sized long-haired white dog came up to me and sniffed and tried to rustle me, but I didn't

really know what he wanted. I just kept sitting there. Where was Mom? Where was Dad? Who were these people? Who were these other dogs? What was I supposed to be doing?

They led us outside to the fenced-in yard. All the other dogs began romping and playing and chasing each other in fun, but I just wanted to go home. I didn't like being here at all. I didn't want to play with these other dogs. I started sniffing around the edge to get away from this place. It wasn't long before I discovered a hole

big enough for me to scoot through. Maybe this would lead me back to my big yellow house and my new mom and dad.

I began to howl as I ran in every direction possible. I didn't know where I was, but I didn't care. I just

wanted to get away from that place. I ran around trees, bushes, brambles. I ran through streams and up and down hills. I ran across fields and through wet mucky stuff.

It wasn't long, though, before I heard someone calling, "Emma,

Emma!" It sounded like one of the people who worked at that place. I knew that name because my mom and dad had taught it to me, but I just kept running because I didn't want to be captured and taken back there. I was running free again like the old days, which was kind of fun, but I was scared at the same time. I was so confused.

But then I heard a familiar voice calling, "Emma......Emma! Come, Emma!" It was my mom's voice. Then I heard my dad's voice from the other direction. It seemed that everyone was calling for me. I wanted to go to my mom or dad, not that other guy. That was the last place I wanted to go back to. My mom's voice kept getting closer and closer. I ended up on a dirt road and everyone kept calling and calling.

Finally, I saw my mom and dad. I was so happy to see them, and I ran towards them. Oh boy, were they glad. They reached out their arms and hugged me and hugged me. They were breathing hard and just

couldn't get enough of me. They kept saying my name over and over again. "Emma, oh Emma." "You scared us so much," they said.

Please don't take me back to that place, I pleaded with my eyes. I wanted to go home with them to that big yellow house and not go anywhere

else ever again.

Thank goodness, they led me by my red leash to their truck. Mom held me in her lap while Dad drove, and it wasn't long before we pulled into the driveway of the yellow house.

"Don't worry, Emma. We won't take you there again." They kept talking to me. "We thought you might want to play with other dogs, but you're just happy being here at home and going for walks on your red leash. That's fine with us."

"Besides," my mom added, "I think you've been expelled. The girl told me they don't let dogs who escape come back there anymore." She laughed. "Our Emma has been kicked out of daycare!"

A New Ad'

It seemed my parents kept worrying about me being lonely because I heard them talking about how they wanted me to have a friend. Not long after I was expelled from doggy daycare, my mom walked in the door with what seemed like a little gray ball of fur. She held it out to me in her hands and when I sniffed it, the live ball

of fur hissed at me, jumped out of Mom's hands and took off running, eventually hiding under the sofa.

This is going to be a new adventure, I thought to myself. What was this animal? They said, "Emma, this is a kitty-cat." I couldn't remember if

I had ever seen one of these things before, but it had four legs like me. It didn't smell like the other dogs at that play place, though, so I guessed it was a different type of animal.

Oh boy, I thought. *What am I going to do with this thing?* We each went our separate ways for a while because I didn't like being hissed at and the kitty-cat hid a lot. My mom held him a lot and he made a very strange noise, like a quiet hum. He did it when she petted him.

They started to call him "Ripley,"

and I clearly was "Emma" now. It looked like he was going to stay and be a new part of our family. I wasn't sure if I liked that idea or not. I had been happy the way things were. Besides, he was different from me.

Ripley began to jump at me and sort of hug me, which was kind of annoying. He did it a lot. Sometimes I ran after him. I tried to get him to stop bugging me, but he would always come back for more. These little spats happened more often and eventually seemed to make my mom and dad laugh. The more we bounced around with each other, the more they seemed to like it. He would hide under the sofa and I would go after him. Then he would poke at my nose from where I couldn't reach him. He seemed to think this was tons of fun,

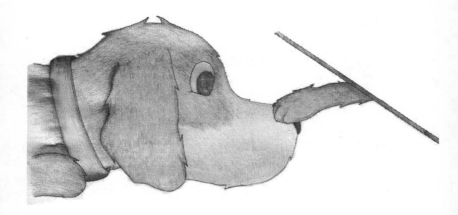

but it hurt!

Ripley had a different routine from mine. He didn't go outside at first. My mom gave him a lot of toys that he batted around and chased all over the house. He seemed to be kind of wild. There was this little gray fake mouse that he really loved.

One thing he especially liked was when my parents got out a little tool and pressed a button that shot out a long red light. They shined it all over the room and Ripley ran after it so fast

I could hardly keep track of him. He ran into walls and whipped around and then ran towards another wall. It made me dizzy just watching him.

Things were quite lively when Ripley played. My mom and dad laughed and called out our names over and over. They seemed so happy, and I was actually beginning to like being a part of the fun.

One thing I really didn't like, though, was that Ripley got to jump on the kitchen counter and basically do whatever he wanted. He was around all the food and I didn't think that was fair because I wanted to be around the food. They also fed him on the counter, I guess because they figured I would eat his food if it was on the floor. And they were right – I would have. Anyway, he was interested in everything and anything – a piece

of plastic, a leaf of lettuce, a fork. He would start pushing it around and eventually knock it on the floor. And then he'd play with it some more until he finally got bored. He was funny to watch. My mom called him "Crazy Cat."

Mom had a jar on the counter where she kept my treats. It was in the shape of a cat. Anyway, when the lid was off, Ripley would reach in there and pull out a treat. Sometimes he'd eat it himself, but sometimes by accident

he'd knock it onto the floor in which case I got to have it. That made my mom and dad laugh – Ripley was basically giving me treats! He was definitely becoming my new forever pal.

My New Job

One day, Mom grabbed my red leash and I thought we were going for a walk. This time she led me to the car. I wondered where we were going. *It'd better not be back to that dog play place*, I thought.

We didn't drive far before we turned into the driveway of a big long building. I had never been here before. My mom and I got out of the

car, and she led me into the building where a girl sitting behind a desk greeted us. After a few minutes, my mom led me on my leash down a long hall. The smells were creepy.

There were lots of people walking around slowly, people in chairs with wheels, people walking with sticks or leaning on weird gadgets. Many people were sleeping in their chairs with wheels. It was strange, and I didn't know why my mom had brought me here. We walked by a room with people singing and a room that smelled like food. I wanted to go in there, but my mom kept saying, "This way, Emma," and would give me little tug to keep going.

Eventually we turned into a room with an old person named Frank lying down on top of his bed watching TV.

My mom pulled a chair up next to his bed and lifted me onto her lap so he could reach me. He petted my ears and my head. He said, "Good girl," over and over.

Frank's hands and head shook a lot. He had a hard time talking too, so my mom just sat there quietly with me on her lap, close enough so he could reach me. It was sort of uncomfortable, but my mom kept holding me as he kept petting me over and over. When we left, Frank said, "Thanks for coming," and "Come again."

I wondered when we were going to go back home because I wasn't having fun, but my mom walked me down another hall. We ran into a little lady named Olga who was trying to push herself down the hall in a chair that had wheels. She seemed excited to see us and she reached out towards my leash.

My mom didn't really know what she wanted, and I didn't either. I mean it's not like she could have walked me or anything because she couldn't even walk herself. Mom gave her my

leash anyway and Olga giggled and I started trotting. "Whee!" she said. "I'm going for a dogsled ride." She kept giggling the whole way as I kept going. It was actually pretty fun.

After my trip down the hall with Olga, my mom led me into a room with a little old lady named Irene, who was lying under a big puffy comforter. I felt a little slack in my leash, so I went for it. I ran and jumped on the bed! I don't know who was more surprised – Irene, my mom, or me. My mom went to grab me to put me back on the

floor – I guess because she thought I had scared Irene – but Irene said, "Oh no, leave her here."

Her comforter was so cozy that I rolled over on my back and she started to rub my belly. Eventually I snuggled up closer to her, kind of under her shoulder, and she got the biggest smile on her face. I think I was making her happy.

It seemed like just about every week at the same time, my mom would grab my leash and say, "C'mon, Emma, we're going to the nursing home.

Let's go make people happy." I grew to like our outings to this new place. My mom seemed to like it and the people we visited seemed to always be happy to see us. I learned which people lived in which rooms and what our visits would be like. They came to know me and my mom by name and always welcomed us.

They would all pet me and talk to me and pet me some more. The best part was when some of the people gave me treats! Then we'd say good-bye and go down the hall into another room. Walking down the hall even started to be fun because when we went by the carts with food, I could sniff around for crumbs. Sometimes I got lucky and was able to grab some.

After a couple of hours, we went back home just in time for my dinner. My mom kept saying all the way home, "Good girl, Emma. Good girl. You did such a good job." I didn't really know why she kept telling me I had been so good when I was just being my normal self.

CATastrophe

It was almost a year now that I had lived in the big yellow house in Maine with my new mom and dad. I was pretty sure this was going to be my forever home and I was very happy. I had gotten used to my routine with my daily walks, my feeding times, and our visits to the nursing home. One new thing that took me by surprise one cold winter night, though, was some fluffy white stuff that came falling from the sky. The first time it happened, I looked up in the sky to see where it was coming from. It landed in my eyes and on my face. It was coming from everywhere in the sky and it was covering the bare ground in white. My mom said, "Emma — that's snow! We have a lot of that here in Maine. I bet you've never seen that before."

The next morning when we woke up and Dad went to let me out into the back yard, all I could see was white stuff and it was deep. I wasn't sure what to do. He encouraged me to go out, but I was scared at first. He put on his boots, grabbed a shovel and made a path for me so it was easier for me to go out. He didn't seem scared. My mom was calling me in her playful voice, so eventually, I tried walking in the snow, but it went all the way up to my belly! After a while, I realized it wasn't so bad. I kept going and then it got to be fun. I even ran in it. Mom would run and jump into the snow

and call me to roughhouse with her. This was winter in my new Maine home and I got used to it.

As Ripley got older, he stood by the door more and more, as if begging to go out. So my mom eventually let him out for a little while on nice days. He would run back and forth between the shed and the house, coming back in for frequent snacks. He did that for hours until by the end of the day, my mom would announce, "Okay, that's it for the day, Ripley. We're not going to let you out at night. There are too many animals out there who might eat you."

This went on for a few weeks until one day, Ripley didn't run back to the house. Mom started calling him and shaking his container of treats, but he didn't come. She called and called and shook and shook, but still no Ripley. It started getting dark and still no Ripley. Our house didn't seem the same. My mom and dad were both much quieter, and my mom even started to cry. I didn't really know what to do to cheer her up. She was so sad. The next morning came and still no Ripley. It all seemed pretty awful. I have to admit that even I missed my buddy. Life was different and I didn't like it.

That afternoon, when I was sniffing around in my big fenced-in backyard,

I heard what sounded like an animal quietly crying. I looked, I listened, and looked again. It was coming from far away. I ran towards where I heard the noise. It was coming from the other side of my fence. It sounded like Ripley. I couldn't jump over the fence because it was too high, and I had never dug under it, but I had to get to Ripley. I picked a place and began digging and digging. I pulled the dirt away as fast as I possible could. My heart was beating really fast because I was working so hard.

Finally, I had dug a hole big enough for me to scrunch myself under. It wasn't easy, but I did it. The faint crying grew closer and closer as I ran towards a very tall tree far away. The cry came from way up. Suddenly I spotted Ripley high up on a branch looking down and looking very scared.

I started howling and jumping at the tree trunk, trying to reach him. I barked and yipped and barked some more until my mom came outside to see what I was yelling about. I kept jumping at the bottom of the tree

while looking up. She ran down and asked, "Emma, what's wrong? What do you see up there?" Then she looked up and we both heard the quiet crying and she screamed, "Emma – that's Ripley! Oh, Ripley!" She yelled for my dad who was out in the barn. She told him what we were all excited about and he came out as fast as he could, carrying what looked like a very long wooden tool.

"Wait, Ripley...we're coming...we're coming," my mom kept saying. "We're coming to rescue you!" My dad opened

a gate and Mom followed with my

leash. Dad put the tall thing against the

tree and started climbing up the steps

on it. Ripley seemed to be hanging on

to the tree with his sharp claws and

looking down towards the ground,

but not knowing how to get down. He kept crying and looked very scared. My mom stood there being very silent and scared. Finally, my dad reached up and grabbed Ripley and very carefully carried him back down the steps. He handed Ripley to my mom who hugged him very close to her.

"Come on, Emma, let's go inside and take Ripley so he can get some water and food." My mom kept hugging him and hugging him. He was still pretty upset, though, and still seemed very scared. We didn't know how long he had been stuck up in that tree or who had scared him so much that he ran up it in the first place. He was really tired and not even hungry. We let him rest and he slept for a long time. It seemed like forever.

When he finally woke up, we all had a little celebration and my mom and dad kept praising me and saying, "Emma – you found Ripley! You found him!" I was quite proud of myself – and happy too – because Mom and Dad weren't sad anymore, and I was glad he was home too. Besides, I was a hero!

Things that Scare Me

I'm not sure why, but certain things really scare me and it's a good thing my mom and dad are usually nearby because they always soothe me and make me feel better by petting me and talking softly to me. ~~Loud~~ Very noises scare me, like fireworks and gunshots. ~~My dad calls it target practice, and~~ sometimes my neighbors do ~~that.~~ what my dad calls target practice.

~~Sometimes~~ Also,

~~Also,~~ at ~~certain times of the year,~~
people go hunting in the woods way
back behind our house. Then I hear
some really loud gunshots.

I look other ~~At certain~~ times of the year, there
are a lot of pop, pop, pops and my
mom calls them fireworks. They
sound like they're from far away, ~~too,~~
but I can still hear them, and they
make me nervous. She holds me and
assures me that everything is okay.

The worst thing that happens to me,
though, is when I have bad dreams.
My mom calls them nightmares.

They are awful. I don't know what it is, but I start whimpering in my sleep and then whining even more. Something bad is happening to me, and I don't always remember what it is, but it takes my mom awhile to calm me down afterwards. I must cry really loudly because it wakes them, and they come running to my bed to hug me and tell me everything is fine and that I'm home with them in a safe place. My dad seems to think that I'm dreaming of bad stuff that happened to me in my before life. I don't know what I dream about – I can't really remember – all I know is that it must not be good.

Things that Make Me Happy

Of course, my walks in the woods with my mom and dad are my very favorite thing to do. I am lucky in so many other ways, though.

When it's cold outside, I love to be inside and lie by the woodstove my mom and dad always have going. It's so cozy and warm. Of course, what's especially fun is that the woodstove is

pretty close to the kitchen, which is a

good thing for me because whenever

my mom is preparing food, I can be

pretty sure she'll drop some crumbs

or something yummy on the floor,

and of course, I'm right there to clean it up for her!

My parents have a little yellow house in my big fenced-in yard behind their big yellow house. It's filled with straw and has a big opening facing south, so when the sun is out, even on cold days that aren't windy, I like to lie in it and bask in the sun. It belongs to me and me only, so it feels kind of special. I like to go there and sleep in it and have good dreams. When I do that, my parents call me their "Sun-bunny." That's just one of the

nicknames they have given me. My
mom calls me her "Little Bumblebee,"
too. And the latest is my dad calls
me "Sister Golden Paws." I like that
because it sounds so soft.

I absolutely love my new home in Maine and my new parents and my brother, Ripley. I've been here almost a year now and it's definitely my forever home.

Acknowledgments

The author thanks Kim Kelsey for her
inspiration behind this story; her husband
for his encouragement; her sister, Mary
Lee Bretz, son, Alex, and Tom Holbrook
and Kellsey Metzger of Piscataqua Press
for their editorial assistance.

Made in the USA
Columbia, SC
07 October 2020